KATIE WOO and PEDRO Mysteries

The Mystery of the Disappearing Treasure Map

by Fran Manushkin

illustrated by Tammie Lyon

PICTURE WINDOW BOOKS
a capstone imprint

Published by Picture Window Books, an imprint of Capstone
1710 Roe Crest Drive, North Mankato, Minnesota 56003
capstonepub.com

Library of Congress Cataloging-in-Publication Data
Names: Manushkin, Fran, author. | Lyon, Tammie, illustrator. | Manushkin,
Fran. Katie Woo and Pedro mysteries.
Title: The mystery of the disappearing treasure map / by Fran Manushkin ;
illustrated by Tammie Lyon.
Description: North Mankato, Minnesota : Picture Window Books, an imprint
of Capstone, [2023] | Series: Katie Woo and Pedro mysteries | Audience:
Ages 5-7. | Audience: Grades K-1. | Summary: When Katie Woo and Pedro
find a treasure map at the beach the wind snatches it away, and they chase
after it.
Identifiers: LCCN 2022041441 (print) | LCCN 2022041442 (ebook) | ISBN
9781484674055 (hardcover) | ISBN 9781484674017 (paperback) | ISBN
9781484674024 (pdf) | ISBN 9781484674086 (kindle edition)
Subjects: LCSH: Woo, Katie (Fictitious character)—Juvenile fiction. | Chinese
Americans—Juvenile fiction. | Hispanic Americans—Juvenile fiction. |
Treasure troves—Juvenile fiction. | Maps—Juvenile fiction. | CYAC: Chinese
Americans—Fiction. | Hispanic Americans—Fiction. | Buried treasure—
Fiction. | Maps—Fiction. | Mystery and detective stories. | LCGFT:
Detective and mystery fiction. | Picture books.
Classification: LCC PZ7.M3195 Mv 2023 (print) | LCC PZ7.M3195 (ebook) |
DDC 813.54 [Fic]—dc23/eng/20220926
LC record available at https://lccn.loc.gov/2022041441
LC ebook record available at https://lccn.loc.gov/2022041442

Design Elements by Shutterstock: Darcraft, Magnia
Designed by Dina Her

Printed and bound in the USA. PO5195

Table of Contents

Chapter 1

The Treasure Map

It was a windy day at the beach.

"Pirates used to come here," said Katie. "Let's look around. We might a find treasure."

"I don't think so," said

Pedro. "And I'm hot. Let's go

get ice cream."

"Later!" said Katie. "First,

let's look for treasure."

The wind blew a paper to
Katie. She jumped up and
grabbed it.

"Look!" she yelled. "It
says 'Treasure Map.'"

"Cool!" said Pedro. "Let's follow the map and find the treasure."

But the wind blew the map out of Katie's hand. It flew around the corner and out of sight!

"Now it's lost!" said Pedro.

"No, it's not," said Katie.
"If we see which way the
wind is blowing, we will
know where the map flew."

Katie looked at the Stars and Stripes. "The wind is coming from that way." She pointed. "So, it will blow the map the other way."

"Good thinking!" said Pedro.

Chapter 2

Chasing Treasure

Katie and Pedro passed a new ice cream shop.

"Let's get ice cream," said Pedro.

"First let's find the treasure," said Katie.

Pedro yelled, "Look, Katie!
I see a paper flying! It's the
treasure map!"

Pedro leaped up and
grabbed it.

"Oh no," Pedro groaned.

"It's not our map. It's

someone's shopping list."

Pedro plopped down on a

bench. He told Katie, "Let's

give up!"

"No way!" said Katie.

"I want that treasure! Let's

keep looking."

They began to run again.

"I see the map!" yelled Katie.

"It flew to that playground."

Katie saw a boy on a swing
grab the flying paper. The boy
began swinging higher and
higher—and higher!

Then he let the paper go!

Katie and Pedro ran after it.

So did six brown poodles!

One of the dogs jumped up and

grabbed the paper.

Then the six poodles ran
away. They were fast!

"Oh no," groaned Katie. "We
will never get the map back."

"Yes, we will!" yelled

Pedro. "We can run as fast

as those dogs."

Chapter 3

Treasure at Last

Katie and Pedro chased

the dogs. Finally the dogs

stopped for a drink of water.

Katie told the owner, "Your

dog has our map."

"Naughty Doogie!" said
the owner. "Doogie, drop
that paper!"

"Arf!" barked Doogie, and
he dropped it.

Katie grabbed the paper. "Oh no!" she groaned. "This isn't our map. It's a coupon for pet food."

Pedro pointed. "I see it!
Our map landed on that
parking meter."

"Yay!" Katie yelled,
grabbing it. "Now we can
find the treasure."

"Wow!" said Katie. "This map is an ad for the new ice cream shop. It says bring it to the store for free ice cream!"

Boy, did Katie and Pedro run!

The owner said, "We want you to love our ice cream. But first you have to taste it."

"It's fabulous!" Katie smiled. "It's a treasure!"

And it was!

About the Author

Fran Manushkin is the author of Katie Woo, the highly acclaimed fan-favorite early-reader series, as well as the popular Pedro series. Her other books include *Happy in Our Skin*, *Plenty of Hugs!*, *Baby, Come Out!*, and the best-selling board books *Big Girl Panties* and *Big Boy Underpants*. There is a real Katie Woo: Fran's great-niece, but she doesn't get into as much trouble as the Katie in the books. Fran lives in New York City, three blocks from Central Park, where she can often be found bird-watching and daydreaming. She writes at her dining room table, without the help of her naughty cats, Goldy and Chaim.

About the Illustrator

Tammie Lyon, the illustrator of the Katie Woo and Pedro series, says that these characters are two of her favorites. Tammie has illustrated work for Disney, Scholastic, Simon and Schuster, Penguin, HarperCollins, and Amazon Publishing, to name a few. She is also an author/illustrator of her own stories. Her first picture book, *Olive and Snowflake*, was released to starred reviews from *Kirkus* and *School Library Journal*. Tammie lives in Cincinnati, Ohio, with her husband, Lee, and two dogs, Amos and Artie. She spends her days working in her home studio in the woods, surrounded by wildlife and, of course, two mostly-always-sleeping dogs.

Glossary

clue (KLOO)—something that helps someone find something or solve a mystery

fabulous (FAB-yuh-luhs)—very good or wonderful

groan (GROHN)—a low, sad sound

naughty (NAW-tee)—behaving badly

pirate (PYE-rit)—a person who steals from ships at sea

Stars and Stripes (STAHRS AND STRYPES)—a nickname for the United States flag

treasure (TREZH-er)—gold, jewels, money, or other valuable items that have been hidden

All About Mysteries

A mystery is a story where the main characters must figure out a puzzle or solve a crime. Let's think about *The Mystery of the Disappearing Treasure Map*.

Plot

In a mystery, the plot focuses on solving a problem. What is the problem in this story?

Clues

To solve a mystery, readers often look for clues. Did Pedro and Katie have any clues in this mystery?

Red Herrings

Red herrings are bad clues. They do not help solve the mystery. Sometimes they even make the mystery harder to solve. Were there any red herrings in this story? Explain your answer.

Thinking About the Story

1. Who do you think was the most interested in finding the treasure map? Explain your answer.

2. What were some of the things that got in the way of Katie and Pedro finding the treasure throughout the story? How did they handle each thing?

3. Hide a small treasure somewhere in your home. Then draw a map showing the location of the treasure and ask someone if they can find it, using the map. Be sure to use labels as needed.

4. Write a story about going on an adventure and finding a buried treasure chest. What is in it?

Follow the Clues!

To find the treasure map, Katie and Pedro followed an important clue—the direction of the wind. They didn't give up until they got to the treasure—ice cream. Here is a fun activity where following clues will lead your friends to a treasure too. You and your friends can take turns hiding a treasure and making up clues.

What you need:

- a treasure—it could be a toy, a treat, or some other gift

- note cards

- something to write with

- places to hide the cards and the treasure

What you do:

1. Hide your treasure.

2. Write a clue on a note card that would lead to the treasure. Hide the note card.

3. Write a clue on another note card that would lead to the first note card. Hide the second note card.

4. Make and hide as many clue cards as you want. Then give the last card to your friends and watch them hunt for treasure!

search inside a book sitting near the back window.
#3

what loo... like a bro...
#5

What do you travel in when mom drives?
#4

Look for a blue sock.
#2

Go to the place where the cat likes to lay in the sun.
#1

Solve more mysteries with Katie and Pedro!